Amphibia Island

Adventures of Eddie Croaker

Revised
Edition

Durwood White

Illustrations by Don Harris

Amphibia Island
Copyright © 2004 by Durwood White
All rights reserved
ISBN: 1-4196-0084-2
Printed in United States of America

3rd Edition, July 2006

3rd Edition
Published by
Wellman Communications
1301 Wellman Avenue, NE
Huntsville, Alabama 35801

Copies may be ordered directly from the Publisher
For $12.00 plus $1.55 for Media mailing ($14.50 Total)
Alabama residents must also add $1.04 sales tax ($15.54 Total)
Multiple copies: Send for discount list.

Order my email and save the tax after receipt of payment:
durwoodwhite@netscape.com

For Judy Taylor

Amphibia Island

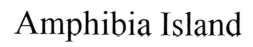

Introduction

This is the story of a little frog that wandered away from his home pond one lazy and boring day. What happened to him could happen to you. You might not think so, and maybe not in the same way, but with similar results. Growing up could be an exciting adventure. But there are rules you must follow, people you must trust, friends you cannot betray, and parents you must obey. Why, you ask? Because they love you, that's why. And love is the strongest bond in life.

Part of growing up is learning to read. When it's raining outside you could open a book and be suddenly transported to a faraway land or even to a distant planet in the vast universe. You should have far less trouble in your schoolwork if you can read. Instead of meeting your friends in dangerous places downtown, you could all meet at the local library. It's a good place to go after school, a place where you can call your parents, a place to do your homework.

As you read this story, don't be afraid of new words. Look them up in your dictionary. Learn the definition of the word; see how the word is used in the sentence. It may be hard at first. But keep trying. Our language is difficult to learn. For two hundred years the language was spoken, but not written down. Two Latin scholars wrote the English language down on paper. They made a set of rules for using it properly. Unfortunately, they used Latin rules of grammar. That's why our language is so hard to write and speak correctly. But you can. It's up to you.

Learn from your experiences of yesterday, set your eyes on tomorrow, and today will be a great adventure. And, so you see, there is no reason to wander away from home. You can wander anywhere you wish in the pages of an exciting book.

And now, let me take you on a journey to Amphibia Island in the South Pacific Ocean.

Chapter 1. Missing Friends

HE WAS A YOUNG frog as frogs go. And it had been only a year since he grew up from a tadpole. He had no name. Frogs were known by their smells. He lived somewhere deep in the Amazon rainforest. Not where the mighty river cascaded down the Andes Mountains, but in the calmer creeks where lily pads and cattails grew. He was a descendent from a family of leaping frogs. A red spot on his head set him apart from other frogs. Somehow he was different from his friends or so the chief bullfrog had told him.

His pond was filled with aquatic creatures. Mostly four-legged animals lived in the dark forest but the frogs knew very little about them. They knew only what the animals ate. It was a question of where they fitted into the food chain. All creatures in the pond learned early and quickly who was friend or foe.

He was a young frog as frogs go

ONE DAY THE OLDER frogs called an urgent meeting of the family. Frogs of every kind in the pond attended the meeting. They chose a big log near the bank of the pond for the meeting place. The chief bullfrog warned each little frog not to venture from the pond, not even to look for the missing frogs. Severe punishment was the reward for disobeying safety rules.

The council of elder frogs thought an explorer had taken the missing frogs. They said he often came to this very pond and took samples of water and tadpoles. But the explorer had not appeared at the pond for two summers. The chief bullfrog feared that the explorer would return. They could not know he came to help them, not to do harm.

"Look out for this man -- He's an explorer, we think!"

The little frog looked out into the deep forest for many days after that meeting. He just sat there alone for hours. Scary sounds caused him to shudder. Was there another pond out there somewhere? Could his friends be there? Who or what caused them to stray from home? Did they really stray from home or were they taken? Was the explorer indeed the one who had taken his friends? For what reason, he wondered?

As night fell on the deep, dark forest and the air became filled with strange sounds, the little frog gained more courage. He was about to do something he knew the elder frogs would not like. The elder frogs had already reminded him about the explorer, and they even told him in very strong language not to venture from the safety of the pond.

Well, he thought, if the elder frogs thought they could scare this brave little frog, they might as well sit on their lily pads and croak. This frog was not about to forget his friends.

The little frog became restless as dawn began to break over the river.

CHAPTER 2. The Wizard of Amazon

THE SUN BLAZED BRIGHT and hot on the summer day that the little frog wandered from his home pond. It wasn't that he wanted to disobey the rules. But his friends were missing and he had to look for them. He just had too, that's all.

He never thought about he danger of wandering away from home. Neither had it occurred to him that not all animals could be trusted. Zneezy, the rainforest dinosaur, was the exception, of course. Still, rules were made for his protection. Disobey one rule and it's much easier to disobey another rule, so the elder frog had said. Soon he would become a lonely frog running around with the wrong friends meeting in dangerous places. One day he might be led into real danger. What kind of danger? Something that he never dreamed would ever happen to him, maybe to others, but not to him. It's much safer to obey the rules, the elder frog warned. But it was too late.

He hopped on the bank and hid his green body under a young banana tree. Snakes and birds preyed on little animals like him, so he sneaked under a fallen leaf for safety. He would not be their lunch today. Sounds of beasts and birds echoing in the dark forest caused him to tremble. He swallowed a deep gulp, trying to be braver than he actually felt. The sounds were so scary he almost turned back. Still, he hopped into the thick forest driven by his desire to find his friends.

A thunderstorm rumbled over the dark forest. Lightening flashes zigzagged across the deep blue sky. Clashing thunder shook the ground beneath the frog's webbed feet. Sheets of rain poured down on the Amazon rainforest. Even the little frog couldn't see clearly in the downpour. His feet suddenly slipped in the mud and he tumbled down a steep slope. At the bottom of the slope the little frog crashed through the side of a thatched hut. When he came to rest, he found himself in the middle of a wizard's magic dance! What he saw would haunt him for the rest of his life, and that could be only a short while away, he gulped, staring at the green monster!

The wizard wore a long green robe. He had flaming red hair. He stood tall and broad like Goliath the giant. The flames of a roaring bonfire cast ghostly shadows that reflected in his eerie eyes. The wizard looked down at the trembling frog and stretched out his long arms, mumbling ancient magic words. The wizard's weird eyes grew red. The tiny frog shook too terrified to even move. He threw handfuls of sparkling dust on the frog's head, then down in the bonfire as he mumbled more strange words. The fire blazed high in sparkling red, blue and green colors. The wizard's eyes grew big, red like fire. He began to mumble sounds like a howling animal. Again the ground shook.

The frog began to feel dizzy. The wizard threw more dust into the fire and screamed three words aloud. His hands raised high, eyes blood red, the green rob draped from his outstretched arms.

The poor frog sat mesmerized.

He found himself in the middle of a wizard's magic dance

Poof!

Something seemed to happen?

The frog's face began to twist and change shape. His height increased. He had arms and legs that stretched longer and longer, no webbed feet or hands as before. In fact, he stood up on two legs like the wizard.

The wizard growled as he stared down into the boy's eyes, snorting nostrils breathing fire. His big stomach began to shake. The more he laughed the more the ground shook. Steam popped up through cracks in the ground. The boy could hardly keep his balance. And then the wizard raised his arms high into the air once more. He spoke.

"You're stuck in time, kid. There is no cure! Ha! Ha! Haw! Haw! Maybe you should have stayed at home. Ha! Ha!

Poof! The frog was a little boy!

The frantic boy ran out of the hut into the drenching rain. He slipped and fell on his hands and knees. The terrified boy crawled like a sand crab racing for the ocean. He never stopped or looked back until he reached the safety of the forest. Only then did he realize his body was different. Why had he crawled and not hopped? Why did he feel so strange? What or who was he?

The young lad was about four feet tall, perhaps forty-two inches. He had hazel green eyes and an oval-shaped mouth. He wore large spectacles that improved his poor eyesight. Rusty red hair matched the few freckles on his face. Other than the confused feeling inside, he looked in every way like a normal boy, maybe eight or nine years of age. Much of what he remembered was like a bad nightmare, especially that episode in the wizard's hut.

Somehow he had to adapt to his new body. His sense of sight and hearing seemed stronger than when he was a frog. And his mind was busy as a bee. He trudged off into the rain flexing his arms, legs, and fingers, not even knowing where he was heading.

He found himself at the pond but saw no frogs. Perhaps they had mistaken him for the explorer and had hidden themselves. He walked around the bank until he discovered the old log where he had last seen his friends. Oh, what where are they, and what am I to do? Then the wind rustled and hair. Somehow he was cold. No matter. It was his body now, perhaps forever. Oh, why had he wandered from home? Then he remembered the wizard's haunting words. *"You're stuck in time, kid."*

He ran back into the dark forest with the rain splashing his face, screaming aloud. "Oh, who am I? What am I to do?"

Chapter 3. The Flying Dinosaur

THE RAIN STOPPED. A rainbow arched across the sky. The sun burst through the clouds drying out the rainforest. A confused lad ran through the forest until he was too tired to go any further. He slumped into a pile of vines exhausted and a bit scared. Over and over he asked the same question. What had the wizard done to him? What? He surely didn't want to meet up with that wizard again and certainly not now. Even in his dazed condition he somehow remembered the prehistoric reptile that often drank water out of his pond when he was a frog.

Think!!

Where is Sneezy?

The snake-like eye was bigger than the boy's head.

Suddenly a big wind slammed in his face knocking him backwards. He propped on his elbows. It was Sneezy, that big sneeze he always had. Phew! And that breath! The pterodactyl sniffed the boy from head to foot. The smell was unfamiliar, and the boy realized that he didn't recognize him in his new body. "It me, Sneezy, your old friend."

Sneezy snorted, blowing the boy on his backside again. The boy sat up, a big frown on his face. "Why you overgrown lizard—its me!"

Again, a big snort. "Okay, okay, so you're not a lizard. Now look, Sneezy I need your help. Take me away from this place—please!"

The pterodactyl sniffed him again, and grunted as if he finally understood. He moved his bird-like body alongside a big rock. The boy ran to the rock, bounced on the rock and leaped on his fuzzy back. The reptile spread his long wings. Up, Up, and away they flew clearing the treetops. The lush green trees of the Amazon looked like a carpet spread as far as the eyes could see.

Chapter 4. Lava Island

THE DINOSAUR GLIDED down from the sky over an island formed by lava, and the boy leaped off. The island caught his attention, but he waved to his friend as it soared back into the blue sky. The dinosaur's loud shriek echoed against the high cliffs.

"I'll see you again one day old friend. Be safe, Sneezy."

The island was completely deserted except for migrating birds living in the cliffs. It was only a pile of lava rocks built up by an underwater volcano, called submarine volcanoes. Hours of walking around the island only made him tired and thirsty. But the young lad did find a rain pool near cliffs overhanging the shoreline. Water trickled through his fingers as he drank. A rippling reflection caught his eye. It was not his face. He certainly didn't look like a frog!

It was not the face that he remembered!

And what were those things covering his eyes? He snatched the spectacles from his eyes. Suddenly his sight became blurry, double-images of everything in view. He returned the spectacles to its perch on his nose. His vision instantly cleared. Maybe he could never be a frog again, he thought. "Oh, well," he sighed. "I'm hungry."

The exhausting trip caused him to lie down on a black rock to rest. His tired body finally settled on the lava rocks. Sleepy eyes fluttered and closed. Before he dozed off to dreamland a strange feeling popped open his eyes. His tongue suddenly rolled out of his mouth and snagged a flying bug.

"Ribbit!"
"Oh, my! What's that?" he screamed, both hands over his mouth.

The sun marched into the west on his first day as a human boy. He sat on a rock musing in the dusky light. The twilight sun sat on the water like and orange ball of glowing solar energy. And the yellowish horizon stretched across the blue ocean. The brilliant colors somehow reminded him of sunset in the Amazon. He was safe now. He settled on a flat rock and dozed off to sleep.

Chapter 5. A Strange Cave

THE LAD AWOKE! Eddie was too excited to sleep. He sat up and looked around. Although it was night he could still see in the moonlight. For some reason he decided to investigate a large cave he had discovered that day.

The mouth of the cave opened to the ocean on the south end of the island. But how could he enter without getting wet? Somehow that problem didn't concern him. And he slipped into the churning water like an Olympic swimmer.

Strong currents grabbed his body, sweeping him toward the open ocean. He dived deeper and swam under the current catching the inflow to the cave. He popped to the surface inside a gigantic room, waves splashing upon the rocky opening. His loud gasp for air thundered through the cave.

He curiously gazed upon strange surroundings. The ceiling of the high cave was open to the sky. He began to wonder how this cave had been formed. His human brain gave him new and exciting insight. There were clues evident to a curious mind. And he seemed to have that kind of brain.

The water was extremely warm, suggesting that the cave had been created by magma flowing from a crack in the ocean's bottom. The molten magma became lava when it reached the ocean's cooling surface. The bubbling-hot lava carved out the cave before hardening. The pressure of steam had burst open a hole in the ceiling located three hundred feet above the cave floor. The moon shone through the hole exposing the stars. They twinkled like little fireflies through the opening.

Suddenly a distant image wrinkled his wet eyebrows. A ship was anchored at the far end of the cave!

Wow!

It wasn't there a moment ago. In his excitement, he crawled upon a flat ledge that extended around the cave like a sidewalk. He dashed around the rocky ledge, and finally boarded the ship without anyone seeing him. In fact, he saw no one. The anchor began to rise echoing off the walls like ghost rattling chains in an attic. The ship creaked and groaned. It slowly moved out of the cave. A sudden chill trembled in his stomach. Could he be alone on this big ship?

In that moment his deep concentration seemed to be invaded by a strange impulse. Maybe it was a voice, he couldn't be sure? These sensations had come often since that awful night in the wizard's hut. Was the wizard here, too? Or had he cast some kind of spell on this ship, too?

Chapter 6. The Mysterious Sailor

A CONFUSED BOY inspected the entire vessel from the wheelhouse to the engine room. There was not a living soul on the ship. He was the only one aboard. The ship began to strangely increase speed. Already it was in the open ocean. Maybe the wizard had cast a spell, he thought? He raced up the wooden steps to the top deck.

The beauty of the night captured his thoughts as stepped on deck. He had never seen the sky from the ocean. Tall trees and mountains hid the sky above his home pond. To his amazement there were two horizons—the sea and the sky. Countless stars twinkled across the heaven like sparkling diamonds on black velvet. The moon glowed just like he'd seen it in the Amazon. Distant memories caused him to wag his tired head. He leaned against the rail, deeply sighing. At least the moon hadn't changed.

A strange little man suddenly appeared out of nowhere!

He stood about twenty feet away, leaning on the rail. The boy blinked his big eyes, even removed his spectacles.

It was not a dream.

A salty sailor stood with his elbows propped on the rail smoking a pipe. He gazed out over the ocean, smoky aroma blowing in the breeze. The boy was so lonely he could not resist talking with someone. Anyone.

"Pardon me, sir. Where is this ship going?"

The little man stood only about five feet tall. His face was covered in neatly trimmed whiskers. A faded, blue cap topped his wooly gray head. The tip of his little nose had a touch of pink. He removed his pipe, gazing at the boy.

"Aye, my little lad. I've been meaning to talk with you. We are bound for a large island in the south Pacific called Amphibia."

The boy was astounded by the remark. "What a curious name for an island."

"An explorer who died two years ago gave her that name."

The explorer did exist! "Did you know this explorer?"

"Aye, I did, my lad. He spent his life exploring the Amazon rainforest, studying the disappearance of the amphibians."

"Amphibians?"

"Frogs, my lad."

"Oh, sir. Could you tell me where the frogs went?"

"But they aren't missing, my boy."

Countless stars twinkled across the heavens

"They aren't? The older frogs thought an explorer took them," e wondered with big, bulging eyes.

The old sailor faced the lad. This boy was truly different. He apped the stem of his pipe on the boy's shoulder. "You, my little lad re one of the new breed of amphibians."

"Me!" he exclaimed.

"You are one of thousands of frogs changed into little boys and girls by a wizard's magic spell, my boy."

He gulped. *Gosh, the wizard!* "And they all live on this Amphibia Island?"

"No," he said wagging his head. "I think you will be the only one there."

"Oh, I wish I understood all this."

"That's the same way this explorer felt, little lad. He wanted to understand why the amphibians were disappearing. One day he joined forces with a wizard in the rainforest, who had discovered a magic potion in a dark cave."

Yipes! "But I didn't drink any potion," the boy quickly confessed trying to recall the wizard's hut on that horrible night.

"Aye, my lad. The vapors entered your lungs."

"How do you know all this?"

He puffed on his pipe. "The explorer told me before he died. He purchased this ship and hired me to transport you little people to other lands. He left a sizeable fortune to pay expenses."

"And what of the wizard?"

The old sailor smiled. "Aye, my lad. He's a spooky fellow all right."

Unanswered question flooded the boy's new mind. But nothing was more puzzling than his own condition: a frog transformed into a human boy without a name or home. Whatever home was, it certainly wasn't the pond from which he came. No, but where was his home? Who were his friends? What was he? And where was he going on this ship? The poor lad was more confused than ever.

Chapter 7. Amphibia Island

THE SHIP CRUISED for two days. During the entire voyage, the old salty sailor told the boy some fascinating stories. Tales of little frogs transformed into humans that he had carried to places all over the planet. Each time he asked a question, the answer seemed to be, "You'll understand one day, my lad." But the old sailor told him he would become more like a human boy with each passing day.

The salty sailor leaned against the rail. His pipe glowed in the night like an ember in a fireplace. He saw the anxiety in the boy's face. But after the countless numbers of boys and girls he had carried to all parts of the earth, this boy was perhaps the best example. The honesty of his questions revealed uncommon maturity. For this reason he decided to reveal a secret to the lad. Words that he had not told the other little people. Deep in his mind he remembered the dying words of the explorer: *"You must find a worthy successor before your time on earth ends."*

The sailor pointed his pipe toward the sky. "See that bright star to the left of the Milky Way Galaxy?"

The boy gazed into the sparkling sky. "That blue one, sir?"

The sailor nodded. "You may need me someday, my lad. Just wish upon that star. I'll know and will come."

The lad's mouth dropped open in amazement. "Then it was you speaking to my mind?"

"Aye, my lad. You are not alone."

THE SHIP PUT down anchor on the coast of Amphibia in the dead of night on the third day. It was a large island, maybe fifty miles wide and twice as long. An inactive volcano rose high in the sky at one end of the island. A waterfall cascaded down the slope, forming a brook that ran through the green brush. The south end was covered with lush green trees and plants. The coastline had no coves for docking a large ship, so they lowered a small rowboat the sailor called a dinghy.

The sailor firmly tightened his hat. He spat into each hand and rubbed them together. "Sit tight little lad." He gripped the two oars and rowed the boy ashore.

The old sailor gave him a map rolled up like a scroll. His bony finger followed a trail from the beach to a village about ten miles inland. He gazed into the lad's eyes once more.

"I think you will like this place. But remember the blue star, my lad. Call on me and I will come."

The sailor doffed his hat, and gripped the oars. He rowed back to the ship. The boy waved and watched until he was a tiny dot on the ocean. He turned and looked back at the island. Palm trees waved in the ocean breeze along the winding coastline. It was so peaceful, nothing like the Amazon rainforest. Nights were so scary and dangerous in that dark place. Somehow he was glad he'd left.

The curious boy walked along the sandy beach with a hint of fear in his heart. Although he felt more at ease in his new body, he still had some doubts. He couldn't know what he might be capable of

doing or not doing. His home pond was never this complex. Maybe it was just that he wasn't brave enough to face the unknown.

Bravery does not always mean to be unafraid. One must be brave to do the right thing, instead of what others want you to do just to be a part of the group, called *peer pressure*. The right action could be to say "no." You will have to make that decision. Try to convince your friends to understand your reasons why. Honesty is always the right action. But your friends may not always want to go along with your reasons. That doesn't change the validity of your reasons. You will have to convince your friends by not going along. They can choose to do the wrong thing. You don't have to. Just say "no." Sometimes a real friend has to say "no" to prove his friendship.

Chapter 8. The Magical Forest

THE BOY ENTERED the tropical forest. Not more than ten feet inside the line of palm trees he discovered a pathway through the underbrush. He suddenly faced his first surprise on this island but certainly not the last. He stood on a red brick road that twisted through the forest. It confused him at first, even startled him a bit.

The lure of the forest captured his imagination

The bricks seemed to have some kind of dark spots. He kneeled and scratched a spot with his index finger. Hummm. Straw? Yes, it was straw! His brain gave him answers.

The history of making bricks with mud and straw went back to ancient Egypt— the days of pharaohs, pyramids, and sphinxes. Slaves usually made the bricks by mixing mud and straw in a pit. The got into the pit with their bare feet and walked around until the mix was ready. Iron minerals in the mud gave the bricks its rusty red color.

He seemed to be in a different land, not Egypt but it may as well have been. The old sailor said it was his home, now. And indeed it was a land of mystery. The lure of the forest seemed to whisper to him. The sailor's promise to appear was indeed strange but no stranger than the wizard's magic spell. Was it his imagination or was the sailor calling him now? Well what did it matter? For now the beauty of the flowers and the magic of nature made him feel at home.

His eyes followed the brick road as he twisted through a tropical forest of blooming flowers and ripe fruit. He didn't recognize the plants and trees growing on each side of the brick road. Even the tiny creatures down in the grass beneath his feet were unfamiliar. But he did understand the ecosystem. This island was swept clean by the winds—nature's way of housekeeping.

As he examined the delicate petals of a purple orchid, he heard a small chimpanzee chattering high up in a tall tree. Funny, the boy understood the chimp's message. The monkey's remarks reassured his feelings about Amphibia Island. It was indeed a peaceful paradise, a place that could be a good home. Just what "home" might be, he wasn't quite sure. At present, it was only a nagging desire caused by his loneliness. Soon he would realize that human emotions were becoming more and more a part of his new body.

Chapter 9. Lily Pad Junction

AT THE END of a long hike down the twisting brick road, he bumped into a signpost that said: "Lily Pad Junction. Population 800." He parted the leaves and looked out on a village spread across a lush green valley. A waterfall cascading down a volcano in the distance had created a stream flowing through the village. Vapors rose from the stream just like the water in the cave. Could this be the reason for the large flowers and fruit in this magical forest? The question went unanswered.

He was breathless for a moment. When he revived his nerves, he pulled out the sailor's map. According to the old sailor's instructions the park should be in the center of town.

He found a pond beyond the town square exactly where the map marked an "X." The entire square was paved with red bricks similar to the walkway that had led him there. A row of quaint little shops lined the square. Gaily people skipped along the sidewalks whistling merry tunes. The sunlight filtered through the trees and cast a long shadow on the pavement. A circle of reverse numbers appeared on the bricks beneath his feet. The boy's foot rested on "twelve o'clock." His eyes followed the shadow up a courthouse tower with a big round clock at the top. It suddenly chimed, but louder noises came the hillside above the pond. He trudged up the hill and found a white bandstand built at the edge of the central pond.

He decided to sample the stuff

People were gathered at the bandstand waiting for the music to begin. Brassy instruments glittered in the afternoon sunlight filtering through the trees. A director stood dressed in a red outfit with white gloves. He raised his baton and gave a downbeat. The band began to play a marching tune. There were trumpets, clarinets, flutes, trombones, one tuba, and a big bass drum.

The boy stood in back of the crowd trying not to attract attention. His foot surprisingly tapped the wooden planks in strict rhythm with the music. These were new sounds that he had never heard in the Amazon. Neither had he ever tapped his feet, except to jump. His marvelous new brain continued to amaze him.

He was so excited that he wanted to sing. But he pressed a hand against his lips afraid he might croak. In that moment another of his five new senses sniffed the air. Taste buds came alive. His nose wiggled. Fresh new smells floated on the air. He turned looking for the source of the sweet aroma.

The tantalizing smell came from a long table set up on the grass to one side of the bandstand. It was covered with bowls and platters filled with fresh green vegetables, salads, fish, chicken, apple pie, chocolate fudge, honey, and biscuits. A noisy crowd of people gathered around the table.

The boy watched them dip into the strange foods with wooden spoons. One kid stuck his finger into a biscuit and poured honey in the hole. Honey ran down his hands and arms as he munched. The hungry boy decided to sample the stuff. But what should he eat? A man touched his shoulder as he stared at a plate of wedge-shaped food.

"It's called pizza, son. Just grab a few slices."

And so he did. *Humm.* Bugs and flies never tasted like this.

Chapter 11. The Weird Soccer Coach

ACTIVITY STIRRED ON the school playground just across the pond. The curious boy crossed a wooden bridge over a babbling stream. The stream seemed familiar somehow, or maybe it was just the sound of bubbling water.

He overheard a group of kids who were talking. Two older girls were laughing at one girl about his size and age. He felt compassion. Was this a human emotion? Her blonde hair was somehow gathered in two pigtails. She looked lonely and lost just like him. His sharp vision caught the glimmer of a ball in the tree above the little girl's head. Without thinking, he leaped high in the air and grabbed the ball. Her blue eyes sparkled. But she said nothing.

Across the way, the soccer coach had watched the lad's astonishing leap. "Humm," Weeby Awphil hummed.

The coach had a clammy face with beady eyes. Black hair, lots of it, matched the color of his pointed goatee. He knew all the boys in Lily Pad Junction, although he didn't recognize this boy. But this lad had something he wanted. Indeed, something he needed, the ability to jump.

Athletic competition was fierce on Amphibia Island. A great rivalry had developed between Lily Pad Junction and the neighboring village of Swamp Water Crossing. Coaches came and went. And his job could vanish, too, if his team didn't win the homecoming soccer match against the Vipers. He stroked his long, black bead, thinking. Mr. Weeby Awphil was a desperate man. He needed a goalie.

"Think I'll have a talk with this little guy," he whispered to himself.

The giggling girls finally left, and the grumpy coach called to the little boy. "Hey, you kid! Come over here. Want to talk with you."

"Who, me?" he asked, his finger pointing at his own chest.

"Yeah, you—come here."

He walked over to the odd looking man. "Yes, sir?"

Weeby Awphil scanned the kid top to bottom, stroking his beard. "Those strong legs of yours are quite a gift, kid. Ever think about athletics?"

"About what?" the boy answered. He had no idea what 'athletics' could be. He had never thought about his ability to jump. It just came naturally.

"What's your name, kid?"

"Uh...I'm sorry. I don't seem to know."

Mr. Awphil puzzled. Amnesia, he thought. "Listen, kid. I'm the soccer coach at this school. I could use a talent like you. Come over to my office. Like to show you how to use those legs."

"Well, I...guess I can. I'm not too busy."

Chapter 12. The Challenge

WEEBY AWPHIL'S OFFICE was cluttered with reports and messy papers. All sorts of strange equipment were stacked in the corners. The far wall across from his desk had photos of past soccer players. One photo looked a lot like his assistant, who stood by the desk.

A strange little box flickered with moving pictures

"Kid," Mr. Awphil began. "We've got an important soccer match coming up next weekend with Swamp Water Crossing. It's the annual homecoming game. I don't mind telling you those vipers are good. Isn't that right, Jim?"

Jim Nasium, the assistant coach, came around the desk. "We would have a fighting chance if we had a good goalie," he replied with a boyish smile.

"What's a goalie?"

Jim glanced at the coach, smiling. Jim had graduated from high school three years ago and took the assistant coach job under Mr. Awphil. The former goalie had a firm athletic body and blonde crew-cut hair. A scar on his left cheek hid in a dimple when he smiled.

"He's the one who guards the goal, knocks away the opposing team's shots to the net."

"Then how would I learn the game?"

Mr. Awphil rocked forward in his chair. "Jim, run that video tape on last year's homecoming game."

A strange little box flickered with moving pictures. People ran up-and-down a field chasing a round checkered ball. Probably a soccer ball, the boy thought.

"Watch the boy at the net, kid."

One of the players kicked the ball straight at the net. The goalie jumped but missed the catch. The ball sailed into the net. Excited people in the stands were clapping their hands, but there was no sound. Jim pushed a button on something he held in his hands. The picture went blank.

"We lost that game 1:0. You just saw the winning score on that video."

The boy scratched his head. "That doesn't sound too bad, losing by one goal, I mean. Does it?"

Mr. Awphil leaned into the boy's face. "Kid. Winning is everything. Don't ever forget that."

The air in the room seemed cold, tense, frightening.

"Well kid? What's your decision?" the impatient coach barked.

"Don't know, Mr. Awphil. Need more time to think."

"Yeah, sure. You think about it, kid. Why don't you come to practice this afternoon?" the coach asked.

As the boy left, Weeby Awphil scratched his beard, thinking. He knew that nobody on his team could defend the net against the Swamp Water Vipers. This kid was his only chance to win. And he was determined to win, whatever the cost.

THE GLOWING SUN sat on the western horizon at the end of the first day in Lily Pad Junction. Dusk covered Pond Water Park in a misty fog. The young boy sat by the pond thinking about the coach's offer. Jim Nasium seemed like a good sort of guy. But somehow this Weeby Awphil character reminded him of a tree-climbing snake that swam in his pond back in the Amazon rainforest. The huge snake had often tried to lure him into danger. Mr. Awphil had all the right words but wrong ideas. For that reason he didn't trust the coach any more than he had trusted the snake back in the Amazon River.

His thoughts were disturbed by a sudden scream!

He leaped into the water

Sounds of splashing water came from the pond. He rushed to the edge and parted the cattails, gazing out over the waters. Ducks fluttered and flew away. He saw the same girl he'd met that afternoon thrashing about in the pond. A ball floated on the surface. He immediately saw the trouble. She must have chased her ball and fell into the pond.

The boy watched the girl as he had often watched his friends playing in the rainforest ponds. She suddenly slipped under the water surface, not once, but twice. He cocked an eyebrow. "She can't swim!" he puzzled, wondering why everyone couldn't swim like he could. He dove into the water and dogpaddled to the screaming girl. She grabbed his outstretched hand and he pulled her closer. With one hand under her chin, he swam toward shore, floating the girl on her back.

She kissed him on his cheek

They crawled on the shore and he stood the dripping girl on the bank. She was soaking wet. The girl shivered with fear and cold. The boy didn't know quite what to do. He looked around and found a red towel stretched over a log, left there by someone. He draped it over her shoulders and cradled her into his strong arms. The drenched boy carried her to the white bandstand. He sat her gently on a step.

"What's your name?" he asked, wiping water from his spectacles with his shirttail.

She seemed to be in shock. Even though dazed, her blue eyes looked into his big, green eyes. Her face blossomed into a big smile.

"My name is Judy Croaker," she said. And then she leaned over and planted a kiss on the boy's freckled cheek. "I live down that street," she replied, pointing.

He touched his cheek, wondering. *Why did she do that?* He took her hand and led her down the red brick street toward her home. As they strolled along, Judy tightly gripped his hand. The boy struggled to say something but had no words to express his feelings. When they reached her cottage, she opened the door.

"Please come in. I want you to meet my daddy. He's the principal of Lily Pad Junction Middle School."

Chapter 14. Picture Over The Fireplace.

A SHIVERING BOY stood waiting in the living room of Judy's house, dripping water on the rug. The large room had strange furniture and pictures on the walls. A chubby man with a kind face stepped to the doorway. He had balding hair and soft brown eyes. He came into the room holding the girl's hand.

"Is this the young lad, Judy?" he asked in a mellow voice.

"Yes, daddy."

"My name is Chris Croaker, son," he said, shaking the lads hand.

"Sir," he nodded respectfully, nudging the spectacles on his nose with the index finger.

"I want to thank you for saving Judy's life, son. That was a brave thing you did."

"She can't swim and I know how." The words just blurted out of his mouth without thinking. His face blushed.

"Judy, get this lad some dry clothes. Check the old trunk in the basement." He turned his attention to the boy. "You're a guest in our humble house, son. Won't you come into my study? I'd like to talk with you a moment."

THE STUDY HAD a fireplace and a ceiling fan. A sofa faced the fireplace. The picture over the brick mantle caught the boy's eye. It looked like the same ship that had brought him to Amphibia Island! If it was, then who was Mr. Croaker? Judy interrupted his thoughts, entering the study with a change of clothes. Strangely, they were about his size.

"Here, son. These may fit," he said, with a finger rubbing his bottom lip. "Do your parents live on this island?"

"I have no parents, sir," the lad replied, draping the clothes over his arm.

"And how did you come to Amphibia Island?"

"By ship, sir. Like that one over the fireplace."

Mr. Croaker smiled as if he understood. "And what is your name, son?"

He wagged his rusty red head. "I don't really know, sir."

The boy's response confirmed what Mr. Weeby Awphil had told Mr. Croaker that very afternoon. "Well, now. You must have a name.

What shall we call you? Let's see…humm…how about Eddie? Yes, we'll call you Eddie. Eddie Croaker. You can stay with us, Eddie. You can live in the basement. Would you like that, Eddie?"

Eddie smiled, tears hung in the corners of his big eyes. His spectacles fogged, and he removed them. "Thank you, Mr. Croaker. Uh, I'd like that very much."

Eddie couldn't know that frogs could not shed tears. Only humans had that capacity. And how would he ever tell Mr. Croaker he was really a frog, when he couldn't clearly remember himself?

Chris Croaker laid his hand on Eddie's shoulder. "I think that's just great, Eddie. We'll enroll you in school tomorrow."

Too many details cluttered Eddie's expanding mind. He had to have some answers. "What exactly is school, Mr. Croaker?"

"Why it's where you learn things, of course."

"What kind of things, sir?"

"Academic things like math, science, grammar."

"And are these things found at your school?"

"Yes. In books."

"Books?"

Mr. Croaker smiled. "All of man's knowledge is written down in books."

"But how…"

"You must learn to read, Eddie."

Mr. Croaker took Eddie's hand. "I've always wanted a son, Eddie. Hope you like the name. Edward was my father's name. He was a scientist who studied frogs in the Amazon rainforest."

Yikes! The explorer, Eddie gulped. "Does your father live here on Amphibia Island, too?" he asked, buzzing with more questions.

"He died two years ago. He's buried in the church graveyard off the square. We moved here when I was just a body about your size. That's why those clothes fit you. My father discovered this uncharted island and named it Amphibia. We came over on that ship in the picture above the fireplace."

The feelings Eddie felt inside could not be put into words. Although there were many pieces to this puzzle, he couldn't quite fit them together. The old sailor was a key piece, perhaps even Mr. Croaker, and certainly his deceased father. The wizard was a mystery all of its own. More thoughts cluttered Eddie's mind, too many questions for clarity. Out of his jumbled thoughts came his memory of Mr. Weeby Awphil. Maybe he should tell Mr. Croaker about the coach's offer. On second thought, he dismissed the idea.

He sighed deeply. "This is all so sudden, sir. I need some fresh air."

Mr. Croaker chuckled. "I understand. Go ahead and look around your new home, Eddie. Dinner will be in about an hour."

Eddie walked out on the back patio in the stillness of twilight. Familiar sounds of chirping bugs and flying insects echoed in the shadowy dimness. Even though he still felt danger deep inside, there was a strange peace about this place. At last he had a name, a home, and a "father," even a pretty "sister." Could these feeling mean he was becoming more like a human, just as the old sailor had promised?

He had no friends, except the sailor, and, oh yes, Sneezy, the *pterodactyl*. Not even the dinosaur could talk like the people he had met at the bandstand. It wasn't that he missed the rainforest so much, only that everything else seemed so…well, so different—these people, this place, his remarkable new brain. Marvelous things entered his expanding mind. At that moment an inner voice seemed to speak. Was it the sailor speaking to him, or his human brain? For some reason, he decided it was time to explore Lily Pad Junction.

Chapter 15. A Mother's Advice

JUDY'S MOTHER WAS a pleasant woman, so kind and understanding. She had cooked a hot dinner for the family. Good smelling food just like Eddie had smelled at the bandstand. But Eddie decided to eat anyway, not wanting to embarrass them. It had not crossed his mind that he might croak. Bad habits were hard to break. Eddie simply relaxed in the presence of his new family. Oh, my, and did he eat! Fried fish, chopped slaw, and something Judy called hushpuppies.

Eddie answered many questions while they ate. Judy's mother asked the fewest questions, caring most that she had a "son" to mother. Chris Croaker talked more about school and teaching Eddie to read. Eddie finally put down his napkin, and thanked the cook for such a fine dinner. It was the first hot meal he'd ever eaten. After they ate a dessert of homemade apple pie, Judy asked that she and Eddie be excused.

Judy led Eddie to the basement, to the very room that her mom and dad had prepared for him. The spacious room was bright and clean. Two windows were draped with colorful curtains. The curtains were decorated with little frog designs. Eddie smiled. There was something special about this family. They were good people. Eddie liked them very much, especially Judy.

A door opened from Eddie's room onto the patio where he and Judy had talked before dinner. The hall door led up a stairway to the main floor. His bed was under a window. It had, what Judy called, a mattress. My, was it soft. Eddie sat on the side of the bed, bouncing his body on the mattress. Better than a bed of leaves in the dark forest, he thought.

"You've never slept on a mattress, have you, Eddie?"

"No. And I've never had a friend like you, Judy."

She blushed. "We'll talk again tomorrow. Good night, Eddie, sleep well."

"Good night, Judy. And thank you."

Judy left Eddie's room in the basement and went upstairs to her room. On the way, she passed by the master bedroom. Judy heard her mother's call. And she stopped, and went back to the room.

"Yes, mother."

A kindly woman turned from the vanity mirror where she was combing her long hair. "How is dear little Eddie, all settled for the night?"

"Oh, yes, mother. He is nice, isn't he?"

"And brave, my child. I'm so thankful he saved you from drowning."

"It will be nice having a brother to talk with. Eddie is so interesting and kind."

"Yes, darling. And somehow I know you will make him feel welcome to Lily Pad Junction."

She bobbed her head "Where is daddy?"

"Oh, you know him. He's off to one of those school board meetings. I wouldn't wait up, darling. I'm sure he'll come to your room and tuck you in."

"Think maybe he will tuck in Eddie, too?"

She smiled. "I wouldn't be a bit surprised."

Judy bounced into her lap like she'd done a hundred times before as a little child. "Mother, Eddie is all alone. What do you think happened to his parents?"

The mother's mind raced back eight years ago, when Judy came into her life. "Only Eddie can answer that question, honey."

"Gosh, it will be just super having a friend to talk to."

The mother wrapped her arms around Judy and hugged her tightly. "Darling, I'm so proud of you for being concerned for Eddie. He needs a friend at this time in his life. I'm glad you are that friend."

Chapter 16. Nightmare

EDDIE SETTLED DOWN in the first bed in which he'd ever slept. The basement was nice and warm, colorful and quiet. So many things were buzzing around in his mind. But he could only remember the last moments with Judy.

The only strange thing about his new room was the absence of stars. He'd always lived outside under the sky. That's why he loved Pond Water Park. But somehow these desires were drifting away, replaced by his new home and new name.

He yawned, stretching his arms. Eddie felt secure and safe. But sleep was not to come, not just yet. The picture over the fireplace revisited his memory. And then Mr. Croaker wandered into his thoughts. The old sailor followed. So far, the sailor was his closest friend, at least he knew most about Eddie's condition. But Judy was different, somehow. He sighed, and then he yawned again.

His body finally rested on the soft mattress, but his mind never slept. Jumbled thoughts swirled in the dark shadows of a distant place. Strange images of people with no faces floated in the darkness. A faceless girl with blonde hair glided through the dream. Out of the shadows an ugly monster grabbed the girl. It dragged her into the darkness, kicking and screaming for help.

Eddie awoke.

Sweat rolled down his cheeks. He sat up. The dream faded, becoming more and more fuzzy. It finally vanished to where all dreams go. He could only remember the scream. He slumped back into the feather mattress waiting for dawn, afraid to sleep anymore.

EDDIE SOMEHOW SLEPT right through breakfast. Mr. Croaker had allowed him to sleep. There would be another time to get him enrolled in school. Sleep was more important at this time.

The morning was bright and sunny, touched with the glow of a new day, and Eddie felt much better today. Still, he puzzled over Weeby Awphil's offer to play goalie. It was too early for him to assume such responsibility. He had only been somebody for one night, just now getting used to his new name. He was not hungry, only anxious to talk with someone. He discovered that the family was gone, everybody. Mr. Croaker had already left for school, and probably had taken Judy's mother, too. Perhaps Judy was in walking distance to the school. "If only I could reach the old sailor in the daylight," Eddie wished aloud. Without another thought he dashed out the door.

Eddie headed straight for the school.

As he walked over the wooden bridge to the schoolyard, he saw Jim Nasium crossing the grassy playground running toward him. Jim seemed to be quite excited.

"Hold up there, Eddie," he yelled waving a hand and pointing to a bench by the brook.

They sat on the bench in the shade of a crepe myrtle tree while Jim caught his breath.

"Something's happened, Eddie," Jim puffed.

Eddie's eyebrows wrinkled. "What?"

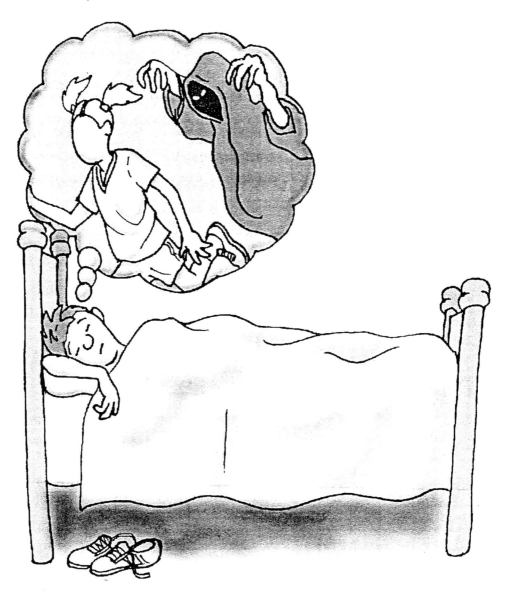

"Judy Croaker has been kidnapped."

Eddie bounced to his feet. "Kidnapped?"

"Somebody left a note that says Judy will be harmed if you don't play goalie in tomorrow's game."

Eddie's face filled with rage. "Does Mr. Croaker know about this?"

"Think so. The police have been called in. No arrests have been made. They're trying to find Judy."

"Something's fishy here, Jim."

He faced Eddie. "You must believe that the soccer team had nothing to do with this. There are many fanatical fans who might do such a thing."

Eddie tried to calm himself. "Guess you better give me a crash-course on how to play goalie."

He placed a hand on Eddie's shoulder. "Okay, Eddie. But I'm as puzzled as you."

Eddie could only remember the faceless girl in the nightmare. And now he knew the scream came from Judy's lips.

But who was the monster?

Chapter 17. The sailor Intrudes

THE POLICE KEPT the news of Judy's kidnapping out of the newspaper. Mr. Croaker had insisted that the police form a secret search part to quietly look for Judy. Jim Nasium and Eddie practiced the entire day at the stadium. Eddie spent that night alone at Pond Water Park before the game on the next day. There were many things that he had to get straight in his head. The sky would be clear tonight. Perhaps the old sailor would come to him. He surely needed his advice.

Jim Nasium had taught Eddie all he knew about guarding the net. Now it was up to Eddie. If only the old sailor were there.

A small man walked out of the mist

He gazed up into the starry sky looking for the blue star. The Milky Way Galaxy spread across the black heavens like a majestic diamond necklace. He fixed his mind upon the twinkling blue star. A few patchy clouds crept across the moon's face. A breeze rustled the fronds on a palm tree close to where Eddie sat upon a stump near the pond's edge.

A misty fog swept over the dark waters. A small man walked out of the mist wearing a faded cap and smoking a pipe. Eddie ran to meet the old sailor. He plunged into his arms and embraced the gray-haired man.

"Thank you for coming, sir. I need your help."

But the sailor's eyes were sad. "Get a hold on yourself, Eddie. I got some bad news," he said gripping Eddie's shoulders. "Lad, Weeby Awphil is holding Judy hostage."

Eddie's eyes flooded with sudden tears. He fell to his knees and wept. He slowly raised his head realizing that Judy needed him. "Sir, the soccer match." he sniffed. "The Amphibians must defeat the Vipers tomorrow or Mr. Awphil is sure to hurt Judy."

"Those are not the words of a child, Eddie. Don't worry. You'll know what to do when the time comes. I'll be at the match tomorrow."

Eddie sighed. "I'll do my best, sir."

The old sailor removed his pipe. "Eddie, my boy. You have been given a new life, a rare gift, indeed. People like Weeby Awphil will be with us forever in this life. But boys like you, my son, come along only once in a while. He is driven by selfish desires. You must humble yourself and help the down-trodden, the weak."

Chapter 18. The Big Day Dawns

THE BIG DAY ARRIVED on the next dawn. Eddie rose early and went to the stadium. He had every intention of facing Mr. Awphil. But he wasn't in his office or anywhere in the stadium. Jim Nasium arrived and inquired of Eddie's condition for the game.

"You're at the stadium a little early aren't you, Eddie?"

He didn't answer the question. "Sit down, Jim," he calmly said staring at Jim. "Mr. Awphil kidnapped Judy!"

Jim jumped to his feet. "You're sure?"

"Dead sure."

Jim gripped his chin. "You know, he has been acting a bit strange these past few days."

"If anyone had a motive he certainly did."

Jim dropped his hands by his side. "You may be right. The police have been snooping around the school campus."

Eddie nodded. "I want to thank you for training me for this game. You've been just swell, Jim."

"Training you reminded me of why I took this job. Just do your best today, Eddie. That's all any coach could ask."

"Coach Awphil is asking a good deal more, Jim."

BY MIDDAY EVERYONE in the village of Lily Pad Junction was at the stadium, including people from many parts of the island. A sizeable group of Swamp Water Crossing fans were on the opposite side of the stadium. Even the old sailor was there as he had promised. The Vipers had defeated the Amphibians last year in a grudge match. The Amphibians had lost both of their goalies to permanent injuries in that game. It was sure to be a rough match today.

The police had not found Judy but Eddie had told Mr. Croaker about the coach's bad deed. Weeby Awphil was now the prime suspect. Because of the importance of the game, they decided not to arrest him until after the match. The police quietly watched his every move. The stadium was covered at all the exits with policemen dressed in plain clothes.

Weeby Awphil paced the floor down under the stadium in a large dressing room. All eyes of the team followed his walk back-and-forth like watching a tennis match. He stopped pacing and gazed at the team for a silent moment. He placed both hands on his hip, scanning the group. Eddie saw something bulging in his hip pocket but said nothing. The coach raised a pointing finger.

"We've got to win this game, boys. The school is depending upon you. Nothing else matters but to win. Win! Do you hear me? We must win!" Weeby Awphil barked.

His devilish face shocked the boys with fear. But Eddie knew exactly what he was driving at. He suddenly grabbed Eddie's collar. "Remember kid. Judy is counting on you. Block that goal boy," he demanded with terror in his dark eyes.

THE TEAMS MARCHED out on the field like gladiators. On the opposite side of the field the Swamp Water Vipers pranced like Roman soldiers ready for war. The Vipers were bigger than the Amphibians, surely stronger, possibly meaner. The Lily Pad boys looked like anything but winners despite the coach's scary pep talk. And none of the players knew exactly what he meant, that is, none but Eddie. But Eddie's mind was not on Mr. Awphil. No. He thought only of Judy's welfare. This game would be a battle for her right to live. If the Amphibians lost this game, Judy was doomed. He's seen that awful look in Mr. Awphil's eyes. And now he was reasonably sure it was a gun he'd seen bulging in the coach's pocket. Was Judy safe?

The noise of yelling fans suddenly rose into the afternoon sky. The game was about to begin. Eddie scanned the crowd around the team beach and up into the stands. Mr. Croaker sat with the police chief. But Eddie didn't see the sailor.

The old sailor suddenly appeared smoking his pipe down near the field sidelines. He doffed his cap smiling at Eddie. The boy formed a fist with his thumb. His mind drifted to Judy as he shook his thumb at the sailor. Where was Mr. Awphil hiding her?

Chapter 19. Play Ball

ON THE VERY first play, the vipers gained control of the soccer ball. Opposing teams took their turns bouncing the ball from one end of the grassy field to the other—stopping, dodging, and changing directions. Nervous tension gripped the players. Muscles swelled with power. They bumped shoulders and knocked heads, zipping up-and-down the field.

Nobody seemed to follow the game rules at first. The referees called several fouls. Nobody had ever seen a player jump quite as well as Eddie; the crowds "oo'd" and "ah'd" each time Eddie blocked a kick. Although the Vipers couldn't score, neither could the Amphibians. Possession of the ball often changed teams. The Vipers tried every trick they knew: Tempers flared up, fights broke out, anger boiled, and sweat poured. The referees could not stop the fights. There were nosebleeds, cuts, bruises, and limps. But nobody would give in to defeat.

The battle raged.

THE TIME CLOCK finally ticked down to the last three minutes of the game without either team scoring. Both teams were exhausted. Two Amphibians had left the field with injuries. With no more substitutes, they had to finish the game without a full team. The Vipers seized the advantage. They moved into a power play, feeding the ball to their best scorer, Spike Skinhead, the bully of the team.

Spike rallied to centerfield. He received the ball with his foot and quickly positioned it for the net with a twist of his ankle. He drew back his powerful leg and kicked the ball.

The ball leaped into the air and zoomed to the net like a bullet. It angled high and to the left corner of the net, probably the hardest position to defend.

Eddie timed his jump until the last second. He leaped with all his strength. He caught the ball in midair about twelve feet from the ground. Eddie hit the turf and rolled to his feet. He took two steps toward the sidelines and aligned his body straight at the Viper's net.

"This one's for you, Judy."

He kicked the ball.

The checkered ball soared like an eagle gliding in the Grand Canyon. The players on the field stood amazed. The crowds sat silent as a tomb. Every eye in the stadium was glued to the ball's flight. The viper's goalie stood in disbelief, pale like a zombie and unable to move.

The scoreboard showed just ten seconds remaining in the game. Down on the sidelines the old sailor lifted his hand and pointed his finger at the ball. The ball sailed the entire length of the field as if directed by RADAR. It crashed into the Viper's net just as the stadium time clock buzzed the end of the game. The silent stadium erupted like a volcano. The old sailor smiled puffing on his pipe.

The Amphibians had shutout the Vipers 1-0!

In the excitement nobody but Eddie had seen Weeby Awphil leave the field. Eddie raced down the sidelines looking for the coach in the crowds. Jim Nasium saw him leave, too, but took another route through the back of the stadium. Eddie ran down the steps to the locker room.

Mr. Awphil was not there.

He climbed the steps to the stadium level looking in every direction. Suddenly someone stood in the shadow of the stadium steps. The shadow moved out into the light. Spike Skinhead walked toward Eddie, helmet hanging by his side. Eddie held his position.

"You beat us fair and square, Eddie. I know something about that little girl, Judy."

Tears glistened in Eddie's eyes. "Where is she, Spike?"

"She's being held at an abandoned coconut factory on the banks of Swamp Water River."

As they talked someone ran down the steps from to the field level. Jim Nasium raced up huffing and puffing. "Eddie," he gasped. "Mr. Awphil has escaped the police. He's left the stadium, too. I traced him to an old, unused back door but lost him in the crowd."

"I think Spike here has just given us Judy's location," Eddie replied extending his hand to Spike.

Spike gripped his hand smiling. "Anybody who can keep me from scoring is a friend. Come with me guys. I've got wheels."

Out on the parking lot, three figures ran toward a yellow jalopy.

A DARK AND GLOOMY building sat on the bank of the Swamp Water River. Dense fog rolled over the swamp. Eerie sounds echoed across the dark waters. An owl perched on a dead branch, his big eyes surveying the swampy hiding places for its evening meal. A water moccasin wiggled along the bank. Mosquitoes swarmed. Fireflies lighted the dimness.

A yellow jalopy pulled up to the building and stopped. Before they got out, Eddie pointed at the abandoned building. He had never seen such a place before. Spike looked at Jim smiling. "Nothing to be afraid of, Eddie. Surely you aren't afraid of ghosts, are you?" Eddie said nothing. Visions of the wizard were still fresh on his mind.

Three boys leaped out of the odd machine. One boy led the other two into the abandoned building. Spider webs hung in every corner, cluttered with trapped bugs and moths. Still they bravely walked into the gloomy darkness. The entire place was really too dark to see. No one had a flashlight. But they didn't know that Eddie could actually see in the dark and had gone ahead of them. There many things they didn't know about Eddie. They were friends now and friendship would bring them closer together. Eddie was an unusual person but so were many of their other friends. Everyone was different. They were born that way. Eddie would learn to accept himself just as he was. They had to accept him the way he was, too.

Spike and Jim stumbled around, bumping in dark corners. They somehow got separated from Eddie. "Where are you, Spike?" Jim whispered, pulling sticky cobwebs from his face.

"Over here, Jim."

"There you are. What a gloomy place. How long has it been vacant?"

"About twenty-five years. It happened when that volcano on the mountain erupted and lava destroyed the coconut trees."

"Really! Hope that thing doesn't erupt again."

Spike wagged his head. "Nobody knows when it might blow again, but I'm not anxious to see it, either."

"Mr. Croaker said a scientist came to the island a few years ago to check on that volcano. He took samples of lava and made some temperature measurements," Jim said suddenly laughing. "You should have seen that special suit he wore to protect him from the heat."

"That's Greek to me," Spike admitted. "My father told me scary stories about that volcano. It blew up during his childhood. It took three years for the forest to recover from the ash and lava flows."

"Yeah, I've never heard that story before."

"Well, it happened and don't think it couldn't happen again—enough of this, we had better look for Eddie...oh, my! What about Mr. Awphil?"

EDDIE GAZED INTO the darkness, somehow able to see clearly. He walked through several doorways covered with cobwebs, not knowing his friends were lost. Deeper he ventured into the dark building. Rows of empty benches filled several dusty rooms. Beyond the next passage he entered a large room filled with long conveyer belts driven by big gears.   A sudden screeching sound exploded   the quietness!

Eddie's hands covered   his sensitive ears. Hundreds of bats fluttered out of the machinery, loudly shrieking.

He heard a muffled noise like someone humming! Eddie curiously followed the sound into the next room.

Sudden excitement flooded his face! There in a musty corner sat Judy!

"Oh Judy, its really you!" She looked unhurt. Her mouth was covered with gray tape. Her tiny arms were tied behind her back. Eddie ran toward her, excited, mad, and thankful.

He didn't notice the shadow moving behind him at first, then he saw it rising up the wall. Eddie whirled around.

"Mr. Awphil!"

A man stepped out of the darkness

"I don't suppose you will understand, but I had to win that game," Weeby Awphil growled.

Eddie saw the gun in his hand. He stood, shielding Judy's body. "What have you gained, Mr. Awphil, your name in a record book? In your effort to win, you've lost everything. Your job, the right to walk free, your self respect."

"Shut up and sit down," Mr. Awphil barked, waving the gun. He pulled out a roll of gray tape from his pocket, and jerked Eddie's arms behind his back. Eddie fell to his knees. The coach grunted, loudly ripping a length of tape from a roll.

A noise!

Mr. Awphil spun around.

Spike Skinhead dashed from the shadows, diving into Weeby Awphil's stomach. They tumbled on the floor but Spike finally wrestled the gun from his hand. Jim fell on the pile. Spike held Mr.

Awphil to the floor with Jim's assistance. While they grunted and groaned trying to tie Mr. Awphil with a piece of rope, Eddie untied Judy.

A sudden beam of bright light flooded the dark room!

Mr. Chris Croaker and the police chief, along with a deputy, rushed out of the darkness. They waved a large flashlight. A deputy lifted Mr. Awphil from the floor and led him outside to the police car.

"You're under arrest Weeby Awphil for kidnapping."

Eddie finished untying Judy's arms. Tape and rope fell to the floor. He lifted Judy to her feet and she threw her arms around his neck. Although he was somehow unable to speak he knew she was grateful he had found her. Eddie's heart pounded with great joy. He was thankful that Judy was unharmed.

Mr. Croaker embraced Eddie and Judy for a long moment as a tear flowed down his cheek. He turned to Jim Nasium. "Well, Jim. I think the Board of Education will be appointing a new soccer coach at its next meeting." He faced the Vipers soccer player. "And thanks for the tip-off, Spike. We might never have found this place had you not warned us. Would you join us for pizza tonight at the bandstand in Pond Water Park? The whole town of Lily Pad Junction will be there, and I think a few of your team supporters from Swamp Water Crossing will attend, too."

"Thank you kindly, Mr. Croaker. You think it's okay to invite the Viper team?"

"Of course. And bring along that fine coach of yours, too."

As the police car drove off into the night, Eddie and Judy drew aside into the shadowy light of the moon. Eddie had many things to tell Judy, but didn't quite know how to say them. Before he could speak Judy hugged him and kissed his cheek.

"Gosh, Judy. I'm so glad you are safe."

She smiled. "I knew you would rescue me, Eddie. I just *knew* it."

"Your safety is all that matters to me, Judy," Eddie replied.

Again she smiled. "My daddy is right. You are a special boy, Eddie," she whispered.

He had felt these strange emotions before. Once when he rescued Judy from the pond, again on that day he leaped up and got her ball stuck in a tree. The way the older kids laughed at her had caused him to remember how the frogs in the Amazon rainforest had teased him about the red spot on his head.

56

A sudden wind rustled Eddie's collar. Judy's blonde pigtails waved in the stirring breeze. Fog moved over the river and onto the swampy bank.

The old sailor stepped from the mist!

Judy was afraid but Eddie knew the old sailor like a brother. He held Judy's hand to make her feel safe. "It's okay, Judy. He's a friend."

The old sailor removed his pipe. "Well, you two. It's time I told you the whole secret. Judy, you are Mr. Croaker's adopted daughter. Once upon a time you were a frog just like Eddie. You lived in the same pond back in the Amazon rainforest."

Eddie smiled. Judy's blue eyes sparkled. They had always been friends.